For my lovely Loredana

First U.S. edition 2019

Library of Congress Catalog Card Number 2019939172
ISBN 978-1-5362-0810-8

19 20 21 22 23 24 TLF 10 9 8 7 6 5 4 3 2 1

Printed in Dongguan, Guangdong, China

This book was typeset in Mrs Eaves.
The illustrations were created digitally.

TEMPLAR BOOKS

an imprint of
Candlewick Press
99 Dover Street
Somerville, Massachusetts 02144
www.candlewick.com

templar books
an imprint of Candlewick Press

By the Light of the Moon

Frann Preston-Gannon

A little frog sat in the nighttime air
in the swamp by the light of the moon.
He sat all alone in the little green pond,
singing his little frog tune.

But all by himself, his voice was so quiet
that he stopped and he let out a sigh.
"Singing alone is not much fun.
What a sad, lonely froggy am I."

So he hopped and he jumped over lily-pad leaves
and into the blue of the night
to find someone else to join his song
and make it sound just right.

He found a friendly crocodile
who was drumming and humming in time.
"My friend," he called, "will you sing with me?
Will you add your song to mine?"

So the crocodile hummed
and beat his drum
while the little frog sang his tune.

But something was wrong
as they both sang along
in the swamp
      by the light of the
           moon.

They found a group of musical mice
who sang, played a flute and a gong.
They made a nice trio, the little frog thought,
and he asked them if they'd sing along.

So the mice sang high
in the dark night sky,
and the crocodile hummed
and beat his drum
while the little frog sang his tune.

But something was wrong
as they all sang along
in the swamp
　　　by the light of the
　　　　　moon.

Down in the murky depths of the pond,
some little fish swam to and fro.
Froggy called down, "Will you sing with us?"
So they added their voice to the flow.

So the fish sang loud,
their voices proud,
the mice sang high
in the dark night sky,
and the crocodile hummed
and beat his drum
while the little frog sang his tune.

But something was wrong
as they all sang along
in the swamp
     by the light of the
          moon.

Some birds flew down from high above
when they heard the hullabaloo.
"We love the song you're singing," they said,
"and we'd like to join in, too!"

So the birds sang along
and added their song,
the fish sang loud,
their voices proud,
the mice sang high
in the dark night sky,
and the crocodile hummed
and beat his drum
while the little frog sang his tune.

But something was wrong
as they all sang along
in the swamp
        by the light of the
                moon.

Froggy put down his small guitar.
Somehow it still wasn't right.
But then he saw a shy little bug
not adding her song to the night.

"What's wrong?" he said. "Why are you so quiet?
Please join in and sing along."
"Not me," said the bug. "I'm far too small,
and my voice is not very strong."

"My friend," said Froggy, "your song *is* unique
and important, like all of the rest.
Even small voices count, so let's hear yours—
only *you* can sing your song best."

So the bug sang out her very own song,
and her small voice carried far.
She bizzed and she buzzed to the beat of the swamp,
and she lit up the night like a star.

Then the birds sang along
and added their song,
the fish sang loud,
their voices proud,
the mice sang high
in the dark night sky,
and the crocodile hummed
and beat his drum
while the little frog sang his tune.

And as the song spread all through the swamp,
each voice blended in with the rest.
Now everyone knew that the song of the swamp
needed everyone's voice to sound best.

Together the animals, the plants, and the moon,
the earth, the pond, and the shining stars, too —
they all sang together their wonderful tune
in the swamp by the light of the moon,
the moon . . .

in the swamp
        by the light of the
                moon.